To my dear friend and artist, Lorna Libert, who said "yes" and brought these pages to life with her incredible artistic talent.

To my friends at Oldfield Middle School, especially Judy and Jen: thank you for all your input, support, and most importantly, your friendship.

And finally, to Old Tess, who gently and patiently taught Betty "the ropes." We miss you more than words can say.

www.mascotbooks.com

Raising Betty

Second printing. This Mascot Books edition printed in 2021.

For more information, please contact:
Mascot Books
620 Herndon Parkway #320
Herndon, VA 20170
info@mascotbooks.com

Library of Congress Control Number: 2021909491

CPSIA Code: PRT0921B
ISBN-13: 978-1-64543-863-2

Printed in the United States

Raising Betty

Sarah Zagaja

Illustrated by Lorna Libert

Today was the day!

It was finally the day we would meet our new friend! All we knew about her was that she would be golden, soft, and fluffy.

We arrived at the kennel and waited with empty arms that yearned to be full. What would her name be? Would she be scared? Would she love us? Would we be able to raise her and teach her to do all the special things she needed to do?

The door to the kennel creaked open . . .

And there she was!
Our puppy advisor, Cris,
said, "We'd like you to
meet your puppy. Her
name is Betty.
She is a very good girl."

She was **golden, soft, and fluffy,** and had a tail that wagged quite quickly. She was letting us know that we were meant to be together.

We arrived home with our new friend, Betty, and introduced her to our old girl, Tess. It was an **instant friendship,** and one that would bring out the puppy in Old Tess.

Tess seemed to understand that Betty had some important work to do and that Tess would need to do her part to help.

Betty was given a **special jacket** to wear that signaled it was time for her to learn. She seemed to sit a little taller and act a little prouder whenever she wore it.

The jacket would someday be replaced by another item—a special harness that would connect her with a special person who was out there somewhere, waiting for her.

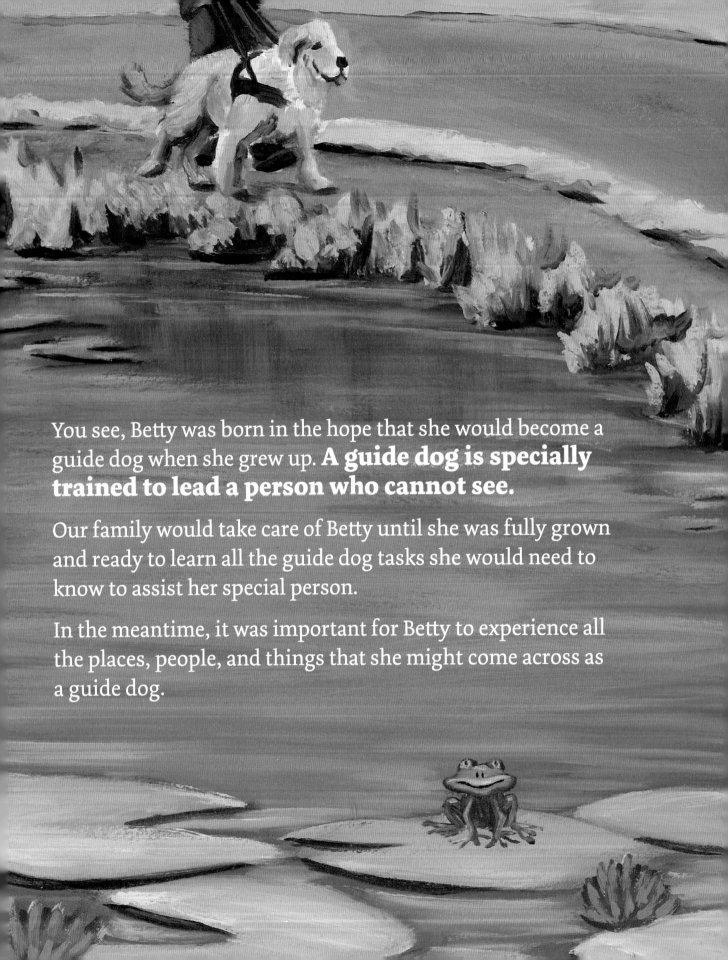

You see, Betty was born in the hope that she would become a guide dog when she grew up. **A guide dog is specially trained to lead a person who cannot see.**

Our family would take care of Betty until she was fully grown and ready to learn all the guide dog tasks she would need to know to assist her special person.

In the meantime, it was important for Betty to experience all the places, people, and things that she might come across as a guide dog.

This meant we got to take her with us wherever we went!

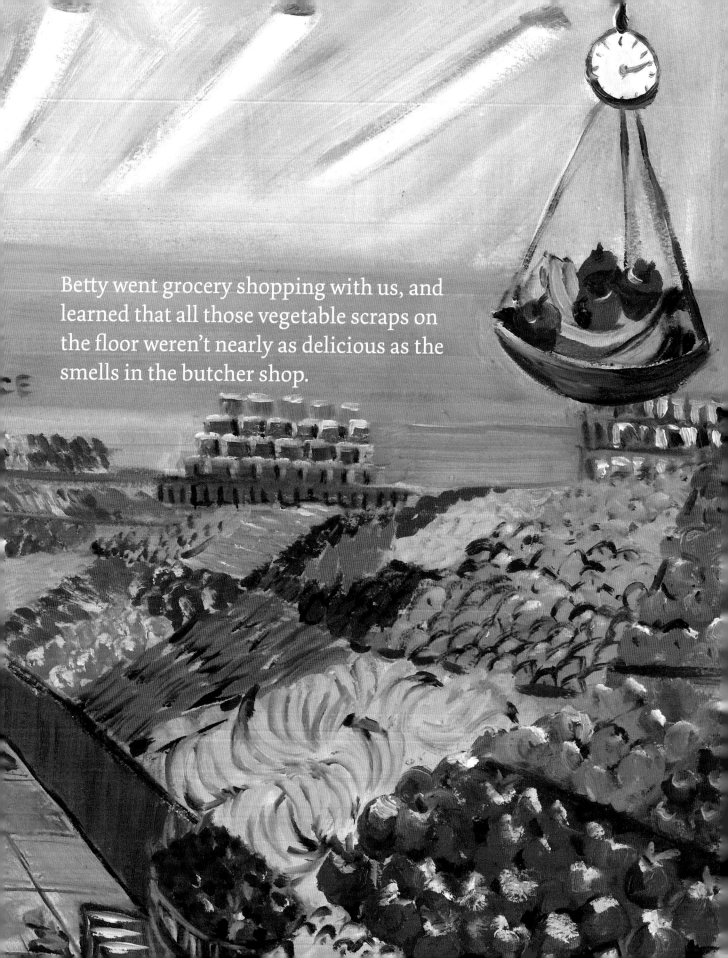

Betty went grocery shopping with us, and learned that all those vegetable scraps on the floor weren't nearly as delicious as the smells in the butcher shop.

We went to the train station, where Betty learned not to be frightened of the loud, clanging locomotives that came rolling in.

She even got a wave from the very busy engineer.

We attended **puppy classes**, where Betty learned to focus on her handler and not be distracted by her environment, including the other dogs that were there.

She learned that romping around
together with her friends had to wait
until class ended and their vests came off.

Betty went to church and enjoyed a nice snooze during Pastor Chuck's sermon. But oh, when the soulful choir sang, she would **sit up, perk her ears, and wag her tail,** seemingly keeping the beat.

But the place that Betty loved more than any other place was the beach. Old Tess taught her how to swim and roll in the stinky dry seaweed, and that the bubble baths afterward weren't really that bad.

As our adventures continued, Betty continued to grow and to learn. She was **strong, beautiful, and fearless.**

We knew our time with her was coming to an end. It was time for Betty to do what she was meant to do.

But how could we possibly let her go?

We loved her dearly, even though we had known from day one that she was not ours to keep. Our hearts were heavy as the day approached when we would have to say goodbye.

When that day finally arrived, we packed up her favorite things and brought her back to **where this story began, the training center of the Guide Dog Foundation.** The Guide Dog Foundation had entrusted us with raising this special dog and now needed her back so her advanced training could begin. Would she have what it takes to be a guide dog? We hugged and kissed her and cried as we said goodbye. Her tail was wagging quite quickly, which told us that she was going to be okay.

We knew she had a very important job to do and that our hearts would mend, but at that moment, life without Betty was hard to imagine.

After several weeks had passed, an invitation arrived. Our whole family was invited to Celebration Sunday, where we would see Betty together with the special person who had been waiting for her.

The invitation meant that Betty had succeeded!

She was now a guide dog who was going to bring love, confidence, and freedom to someone who needed her the most. Her special person was named Miss Conde, and she was from New York City.

We cried at Celebration Sunday, but they were tears of happiness!

Before our eyes we saw what
was meant to be. Betty and Miss
Conde—what a team! Miss Conde
needed Betty to guide her across the Big
Apple on foot, by rail, and by bus.

**What wonderful adventures awaited
our strong, beautiful, and fearless girl!**

Our hearts were full that day, but our job wasn't done. . . because sitting back in the kennel was another puppy that was **golden, soft, and a little less fluffy,** waiting to meet us.

Author's Note

Betty is still faithfully guiding Miss Conde across New York City. Miss Conde lives more than eight miles from where she works and is grateful to have the assistance of her dear Betty in making the daily trek along some of the busiest streets in America. If you are visiting New York City, perhaps you will be lucky enough to see them! But remember, do not call out to Betty or any other working guide or service dog. They need to focus on the task at hand.

By the way, did you know that when training puppies, the raisers use treats to enforce good behavior? Betty's favorite treats we used during her training were small biscuits.

Can you find Betty's biscuits hidden in the pages of her story?